D0311780
WEXFORD LIBRARY SERVICE

raintree
a Capstone company — publishers for children

Raintree is an imprint of Capstone Global Library Limited, a company incorporated in England and Wales having its registered office at 264 Banbury Road, Oxford, OX2 7DY – Registered company number: 6695582

www.raintree.co.uk
myorders@raintree.co.uk

Copyright © 2021 DC Comics
BATMAN and all related characters and elements are trademarks of and © DC Comics. (s21)

All rights reserved. No part of this publication may be reproduced in any form or by any means (including photocopying or storing it in any medium by electronic means and whether or not transiently or incidentally to some other use of this publication) without the written permission of the copyright owner, except in accordance with the provisions of the Copyright, Designs and Patents Act 1988 or under the terms of a licence issued by the Copyright Licensing Agency, Barnard's Inn, 86 Fetter Lane, London, EC4A 1EN (www.cla.co.uk). Applications for the copyright owner's written permission should be addressed to the publisher.

Designed by Hilary Wacholz
Contributing artists: Luciano Vecchio, Dan Schoenin, Erik Doescher, Mike DeCarlo, Lee Loughridge and Leonel Castellani
Printed and bound in India

978 1 3982 0606 9 (hardback)
978 1 3982 0607 6 (paperback)

British Library Cataloguing in Publication Data
A full catalogue record for this book is available from the British Library.

WRITTEN BY
MATTHEW K. MANNING

ILLUSTRATED BY
DARIO BRIZUELA

Victor Stone is running faster than he has ever run in his life. He reaches out as far as he can. His fingers stretch. He catches the ball!

Vic runs the ball in for a touchdown. Because of Vic, his American football team wins the game. His teammates lift him up onto their shoulders.

Vic steals a look into the happy crowd. The seat saved for his dad is empty. It's always empty.

7
59
60

Suddenly, Batman's famous jet, the Batwing, streaks overhead. Superman and Wonder Woman fly alongside it.

FWOOSH!

"Wonder where they're headed?" asks Vic's friend, Ronnie. "You think your dad might know why they –"

But Vic is no longer there. He is already on his way to S.T.A.R. Labs.

"Dad, you won't believe who I just saw!" Vic says, bursting through the lab's door.

"Not now, Victor," says Dr Silas Stone. He doesn't look up from his computer screen. Dr Stone is a busy man. He's one of the lead scientists at S.T.A.R. Labs. Studying people like Superman and Wonder Woman is his full-time job.

"But at my game I –"

Dr Stone looks up. “Ah,” he says. “Your game. I’m sorry, son. I just didn’t have time.”

Vic already knows his dad thinks American football is a waste of time. He's never understood that sport is part of who Vic is. He loves the action. He loves working with a team.

He's about to say something when a red light begins to flash. A **siren** goes off. Another scientist calls for help.

"Go home, Victor," Dr Stone says.

Vic doesn't listen. Instead, he follows his father.

One of the other scientists, Dr Sarah Charles, points to a mysterious alien device. They call it a Mother Box. "It just started glowing!" she says.

BOOOOOOOOM!

The building shakes. A **portal** appears above the Mother Box. Winged soldiers fly through. Drool drips from their large, sharp teeth. Their golden claws shine.

They swarm through the lab and into the city. The Mother Box explodes. Then the portal closes.

Dr Charles finds Vic lying on the lab's floor.

"Get him to the Red Room!" yells Dr Stone. His voice is full of panic. "Hurry!"

Vic doesn't remember what happens next. He spends most of the time asleep. He can hear voices, though. They sound like they're arguing. Some sound afraid.

When Vic tries to open his eyes, he only sees ones and zeroes. The numbers get smaller and smaller. They begin to flow together and form a shape in his mind. They become a dark planet.

It's a place of evil, of sadness and **despair**. Somehow, he knows its name – Apokolips.

The planet shifts into a man with glowing red eyes. It is Darkseid, the greatest evil in the universe.

Vic wakes up alone in a hospital bed. Strangely, nothing hurts. He feels great, in fact. He feels like he's never had this much energy in his life. He stands up and looks in the mirror.

What he see is something more machine than man.

"Victor?" says a familiar voice.

Vic spins to see his father.

“What did you do to me?”

Vic shouts.

His father tries to explain. Most of Vic's body was destroyed when the Mother Box blew up. They used experimental **technology** to save his life.

Pain pierces Vic's head. Numbers begin to rush in front of his now-**cybernetic** eye.

"Victor, try to calm down," says Dr Stone. "Your brain is still adjusting to your new robotic body."

Vic looks at his dad. Then he jumps out of the window.

2548365

The road crunches beneath Vic's feet. Broken glass rains down around him. He jumped from the building's fifth storey, but he didn't even feel the fall.

Suddenly, an alien from the lab swoops in. Vic's **electronic** eye scans the creature. He learns it is a Parademon, one of Darkseid's mindless servants from the planet Apokolips.

Vic's arm transforms into a **sonic** cannon. The Parademon is surprised. But not as surprised as Vic!

The alien turns and flees. Vic raises his arm and takes aim.

A winged shadow falls over Vic. But this one does not belong to a Parademon. This shadow belongs to Batman!

Before Batman can say anything, there's a huge rumble.

BOOOOOOOOM!

A new portal opens in the sky. More Parademons pour out. They are followed by Darkseid. He stands on two small discs that **hover** in the air.

"People of Earth," he roars. "It is time to accept your new lord and master – Darkseid!"

Vic scans the portal. He learns it is called a Boom Tube. But he also learns that there's a way to stop it. The Mother Box has given him the ability to control the alien technology.

"I think I can **hack** into the Boom Tube," Vic says. "But I need a **distraction**!"

"We can help," says Batman, stepping forward. "My friends will provide your distraction." He points to the sky.

Superman and Wonder Woman swoop in overhead. They shoot straight towards the villain!

It sounds like thunder as the heroes hammer Darkseid with their fists.

“Yeah,” says Vic. “That should do the trick.” Then he closes his eyes and concentrates. He wills himself to use the powers from the Mother Box. Ones and zeroes flash through his mind. His head begins to hurt.

In the sky, Darkseid blasts his Omega beams at Wonder Woman and Superman. The heroes are flung backwards.

Meanwhile, numbers begin to form an image in Vic's mind. Vic sees a Boom Tube. Then he sees many. Darkseid has opened these portals all over the world!

Vic's eyes snap open. "NOW!" he yells.

Superman and Wonder Woman punch Darkseid in the chest at the same time.

Darkseid falls backwards. A hover disc slips off of one of his feet.

"No!" Darkseid yells.

Vic focuses again. He pictures the Boom Tubes clearly in his mind. Then he clenches his fists. The Boom Tubes close, taking Darkseid with them.

"Victor!" Dr Stone shouts from down the street. "Victor, where are you?"

"I'm okay, Dad," Vic says. His father runs towards him.

Vic looks at Batman. "The Boom Tubes are shut for good," he says. "I hacked the system so Darkseid can't reopen them."

The Dark Knight nods and then steps back into the alley.

"Let's get you to the lab," says Dr Stone.

"Not yet, Dad," Vic says. "There are Parademons still out there. I've got to go to work."

Vic sees Batman smile from the shadows.

From that day on, things are different. Vic can't play American football. He rarely has time to see his friends. He spends most of his days at S.T.A.R. Labs.

But when trouble arises, Vic truly gets to be himself. That's when he gets to be part of a team again – the Justice League.

He is the hero known as . . .

. . . Cyborg!

EVERYTHING ABOUT...

CYBORG™

REAL NAME: VICTOR STONE

ROLE: CRIME FIGHTER

BASE: DETROIT, MICHIGAN

Victor Stone was an ordinary human. Then an accident turned him into a half-man, half-machine known as Cyborg. His powers give him superhuman strength, stamina and computer skills.

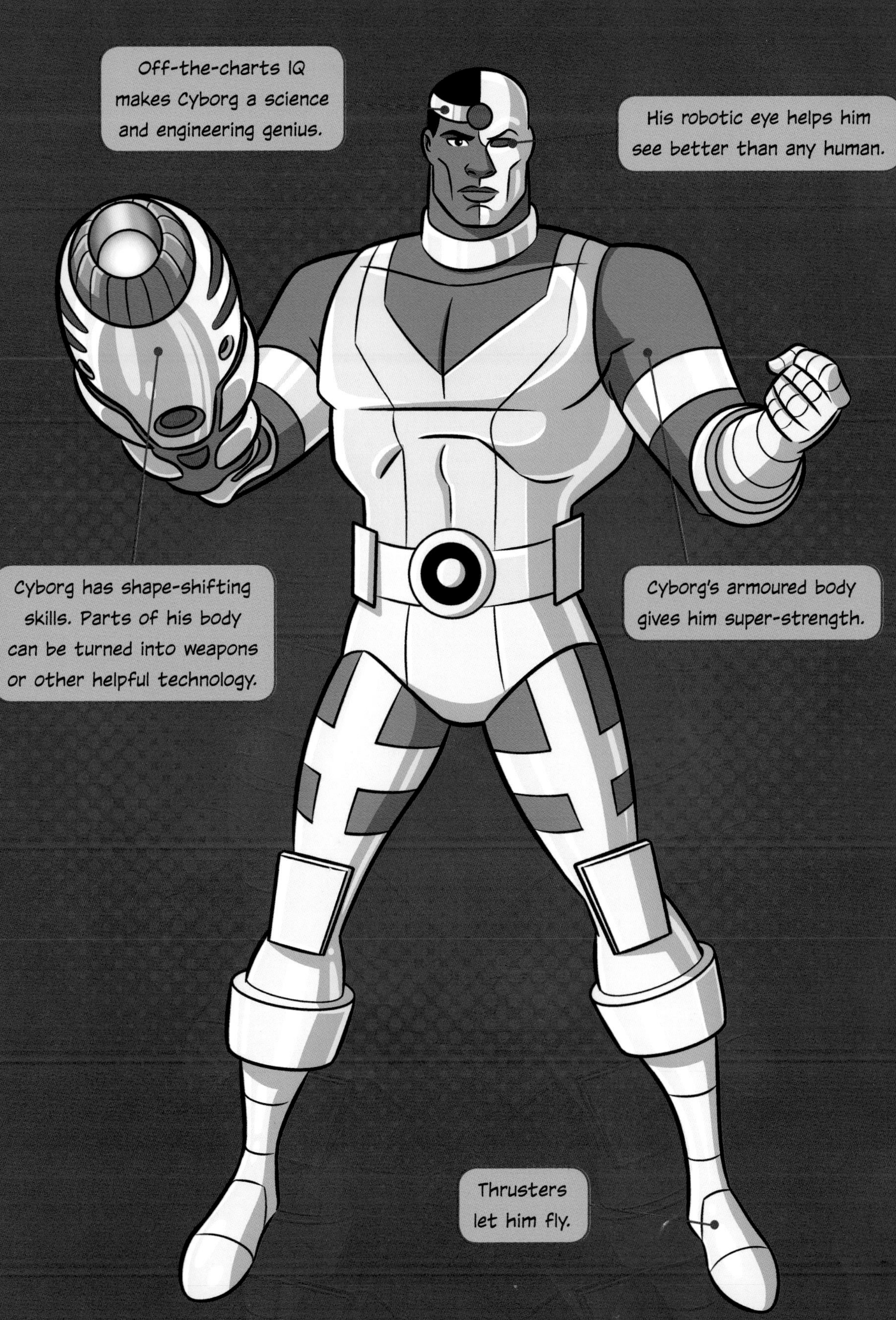
Off-the-charts IQ makes Cyborg a science and engineering genius.
His robotic eye helps him see better than any human.
Cyborg has shape-shifting skills. Parts of his body can be turned into weapons or other helpful technology.
Cyborg's armoured body gives him super-strength.
Thrusters let him fly.

MATTHEW K. MANNING has written comics and books starring Batman, Superman, Wonder Woman, Green Lantern, the Flash and even Scooby-Doo. Some of his more recent works include *Batman/Teenage Mutant Ninja Turtles Adventures*, *Marvel Action: Avengers* and the Raintree chapter book series Xander and the Rainbow-Barfing Unicorns. He lives in Asheville, North Carolina, USA, with his wife Dorothy and his two daughters, Lillian and Gwendolyn.

THE ILLUSTRATOR

DARIO BRIZUELA was born in Buenos Aires, Argentina, and as a teen he began studying in an art school – doing drawing, sculpture, painting and more. After discovering super hero comic books, his goal was draw his favourite characters. He has worked for major publishers like Dark Horse Comics, IDW, Viz Media, DC Comics and Marvel Comics. He has also worked for Hasbro and LEGO. Star Wars Tales, Super Friends, Justice League Unlimited and Scooby-Doo are just a few of his artistic contributions.

cybernetic something that is artificial and controlled by computers

despair the complete loss of hope

distraction something that draws attention away from something else

electronic powered by electricity; electricity is a form of energy

hack to break into computer systems

hover to remain in one place in the air

portal a large, impressive opening or entrance

siren a device that makes a loud sound

sonic having to do with sound waves

technology the use of science to do practical things, such as designing complex machines

DISCUSSION QUESTIONS

Write down your answers. Refer back to the story for help.

QUESTION 1.

Vic woke up to find himself completely changed. Make a list of his new abilities as Cyborg.

QUESTION 2.

Vic's father studies people like Superman and Wonder Woman. Think of a cool job (real or made-up) that you would like to have.

QUESTION 3.

On pages 32-33, Superman and Wonder Woman are fighting Darkseid together. Think of a time when you've worked with another person. Did it work better than doing it by yourself?

QUESTION 4.

Who is your favourite Justice League super hero? Why?

READ THEM ALL!!

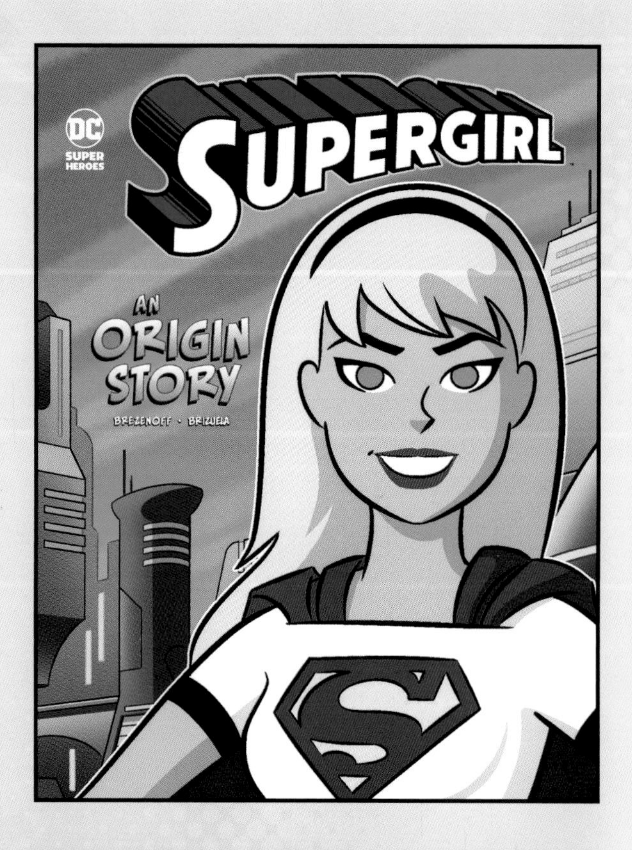

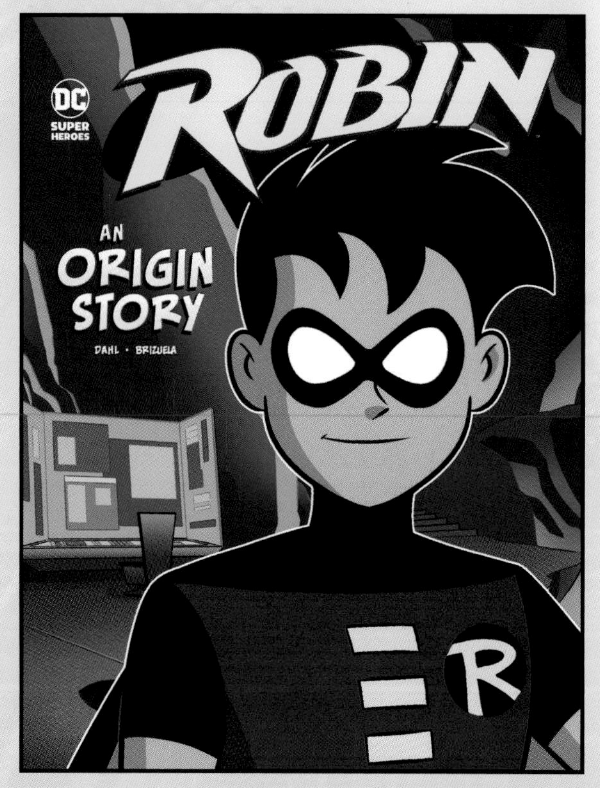

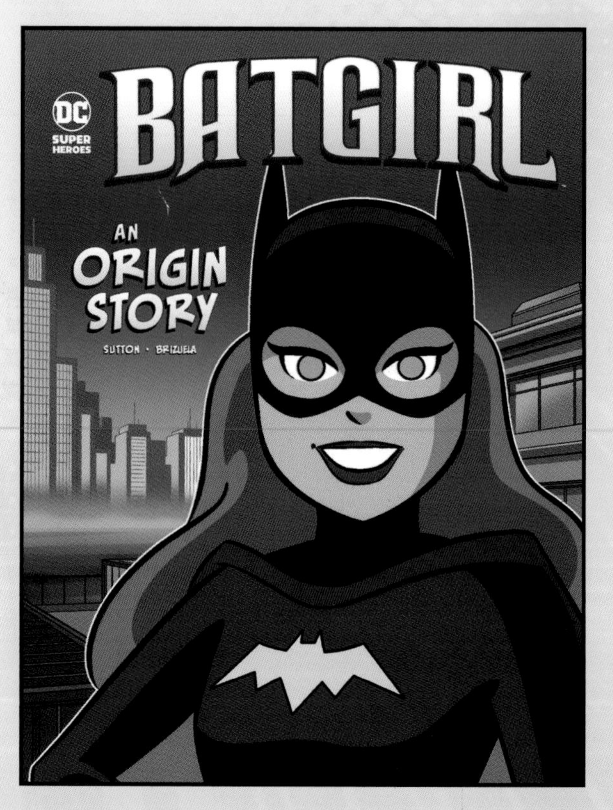

CIRCULATING STOCK WEXFORD PUBLIC LIBRARIES
BLOCK LOAN
BUNCLODY
ENNISCORTHY
GOREY
MOBILE NORTH
MOBILE SOUTH
NEW ROSS
WEXFORD